Jacob Marley

or the Heretofore Unknown
Phantasmagorical Experience of
Ebenezer Scrooge's
Valued Friend and Deceased Partner,
Jacob Marley, Esq.

From the pen of
Ken Lansdowne

Including 10 B&W facsimile etchings

Passage I

Jacob Marley was dead.

As dead as a previous chronicler had made him out to be. As dead as the proverbial doornail, or coffin nail, or any other hand wrought utensil of the ironmongers trade. A ha'penny nail, perhaps?

2
Jacob Marley

Jacob, having returned that very night from his sojourn among the existant beings, was sorely drained and exhausted; for it did use much of a spirit to appear to the living, depleting them mightily of their essence. Jacob now sat in front of those he did entreat and cajole on behalf of his friend Ebenezer Scrooge.

The place he was settled in had no partitions, and was diaphanous and cloud like in its aspect, swirling with mist and vapors, just then laying low upon the floor. There were no walls or limits to surround him. The area was also empty of artifacts. No furniture, save the single ottoman Jacob sat upon. An uncomfortable arrangement of wooden pieces, if ever there was one, it was a single board without back or side and covered by a thin layer of horsehair with a bilious woven floral topping. Its gaudy gimp and tarnished metallic tassels profusely attached all round did nothing to guarantee a bodies comfort.

He heard a snap, nay, a loud clap of thunder, and looked wearily up. "Well, Jacob..." His superiors voice echoed in his ears, "...has your mission with the human, Scrooge, resulted in the desired conclusion?"

Thereupon Jacob took note of a strange and wondrous phenomenon. The vapor that had lately hung at the floor now was swirling and reaching higher and higher, filling the space around him with deep arches and shadows. The haze was moving, forming into amorphous shapes of urns and figure. And before him there was a vague human shape. A shoulder, a thigh, a head. It further took on an aspect of colour that echoed the tone being used by the speaker. First blue, then pale green, then emerald, all shadow, all moving and diffusing, showing only a small piece of his person at a time. Jacob was able to make out the shape of an all seeing eye and a furrowed brow as the voice inside his head asked its questions. This vision would last a moment then break up and disappear again into the quickly moving smoke and fog

FILLING THE SPACE WITH DEEP ARCHES AND SHADOWS

"I know not," Jacob replied, as he removed the folded kerchief that had bound his head and chin. "He was a stubborn and recalcitrant old sinner. At first he thought me merely an irritant. An undone potato, if you will. But I did afright him mightily and I believe he came to consider us. We shall know more when the spirits I foretold him do return from their tasks. Again, I thank ye for the opportunity you have granted me, and through my offices, him."

The fog formed a side of a face, old, wise, bearded with long floating hair.

"And how did you find your old partner, Jacob? Was there much change on the corporal plain in these seven years you have been among us?"

"All seems desolate and empty there, dear apparition. Dark and forbidding. Ebenezer has sold or disposed of all of my possessions. My old rooms are as empty as a poor man's pockets. He was, it seems, enamored with none of it."

"Merely things. Do you still hold an attachment to these gee-gaws, Jacob?"

Thinking he heard irritation in the voice, and indeed the colour of the shadowy mist had turned a deep purple, Jacob quickly replied, "No. No. That is not the reason I bring it up. I mention it because it simply proves Scrooge had no loving attachment for me."

"And that is not true of you, is it, Jacob Marley?"

"That is accurate, good specter." Jacob watched his long thin fingers knit and purl in his lap. "Ebenezer was, in my previous aspect, my warm friend. I did have great affection for the man. He knew not my feelings, and the things I most regret are the things left unsaid between us."

"This is why you interceded on his behalf then? This amatory effusion of yours for Ebenezer Scrooge? Explain yourself, Jacob Marley."

"When living my fleshly span I was mightily afeared of the aftereffect of admitting my personal truth. Now that I am spirit I no longer worry at the results of my confession, and am relieved, my lord, at the loss of the burden. But I myself am less able to explain than anyone else. I know that since I was born into that world, my heart was a question that no other heart did solve. Now staring at the ruins that became my life I am insensible at the torrent that bore me off with my shattered hopes. Was this affliction the affliction of nature? I know not. I only know that what I felt for Ebenezer Scrooge was against religion and law..."

"And what of nature?"

"Not nature, dear specter. It was, I am sure, my own nature, as natural to me as breathing. As natural as being right handed. As natural as my indifference to the other sex."

"Then you lived that previous existence as a Uranian? You were a stranger among your own? A Sodomite?" Jacob heard the bluntly put question but felt no censure from it. The voice only asked for an answer, its tone neither condemning nor acquiescing.

"True enough. I was throughout that life sorely vexed by a hermophrodism of my soul. I searched high and very low for a Socratic love of my own. I know clearly that I harboured a thwarted, frustrated, impossible partiality for Ebenezer Scrooge. That he never did return my affect for him was, like the penitent upon a prison treadmill, my punishment and my cross. It is, I fear, the reason I carry these ponderous iron chains upon my person. They are forged from that veiled secret that did fester and reside inside me. It caused me much anguish and turmoil as I trod London's byways and alleys, streets and boulevards, searching for another like myself. But it was not to be. I found many willing to spend time with me, but none would stay, none would return my affection. I was doomed to remain alone in my horrible existence."

The misty swirling color had turned again. This time ranging from a soft pink to an angry red. Was it a warning that Jacob had trod on unwelcome territory? But Jacob could not be halted in this. He sank to his knees and pleaded with the spirit, continuing again and again to profess his guilt and torment. "Good spirit, I was made to feel by my own that I was a disseminator of filth and dirt vomited up from the foul pit of my own sin and anguish. Oh! Woe! Must I continue to pay for a sin not of my making? Is this to be my fate forever more?"

The voice roared in Jacob's head. "Not of *your* making? Not *yours*? Not mine either. You were cast out by society, not by nature. The sin is yours, Jacob Marley. Look to yourself for any solace you might seek."

The mist swirled, turned white and was no more, only a slight fog floating now mild and calm over Jacob Marley's prone and prostrate body, his sobs the only sound in the cold unforgiving echoing space.

Passage II

Still lying with his head buried upon his folded arms, Jacob Marley felt a soft hand laid on his shoulder. Looking to find the culprit he saw the first of the beneficent spirits sent to facilitate the reclamation of Ebenezer Scrooge. Sitting, Jacob said, "Ah, old friend, my dear Ambroise, you have returned from your duty of this evening. How went it?"

Ambroise, a small mature man with a child like demeanor smiled beatifically. "At first I was convinced that Mr. Scrooge was beyond redemption, but toward the end of our time together there were enough cracks in the old transgressor's lobster like shell that I have hope the second ghost who shall visit him this night will further our cause."

"And why do you wear your extinguisher-cap so low upon your brow?"

"Scrooge, to be rid of the visions he had seen did use it to put out my light..." He reached up and raised it some. Small beams of light shot from under it and lit the area around them with in a soft glow. "But it was not my doing as to what he saw, so he did accuse the wrong vessel. I was but the conduit." The ghost looked on Jacob with a knowing glance. "But what of you, Jacob? Are you not buoyed by this news of your old acquaintance?"

"Aye, Ambroise, well enough."

Ambroise slid his white frizzed head from side to side and laid a finger beside his nose. "Then, my dear, I needs know the reason for the long hanging chin and sorrowful bearing? You show the same suffering demeanor as a man doomed to the gallows on the coming morn."

"Doomed to be sure. I have been sentenced to an ageless eternity of this same hopeless wandering I have endured for these last seven years. I am convinced there will be no end, no redemption for mine own soul. I have nothing to look forward too but more of this torture, this relentless agony..." Jacob picked up the chain hanging from his waist and rattled it. "... this encumbrance from the dark depths of Satan's domain."

"Not true. I myself have witnessed the saving of many souls from their unhappy fetters. It can be done I am sure. There is but a simple solution."

"Solution, Ambroise?" Jacob looked upon him hopefully. "What ho? What say you it to be?"

Jacob Marley

"You have previously been apprised by the master, Jacob. You are aware of the cure for your infirmity. He said it clearly. He told you to look to your own self. Is that not clear enough for you?"

Jacob looked disconsolate. "Ambroise, woe unto me, I am unable to understand what he has meant. I am already repentant. I am surely sorrowful. I am certainly accursed. Is this not enough? Is this not what he seeks?"

"As you are still chained and wandering like the Jews in the deserts of Canaan then I must surmise it is not. What else do you have?"

"I know not." Jacob set out to wail a mournful bawl at his foul predicament. "Halt, good spirit..." Ambroise stayed him. "Perhaps there is a way to find a reprieve. I have a notion, a possible solution, to your quest."

"Pray, do not hold it from me. What is it?"

"What if I were to do for you what I have but a moment ago accomplished for Ebenezer Scrooge? What if I were to guide you on a similar journey into your own past. To show you what transpired and chance upon the exact thing you seek to proffer for your salvation."

"Do you suppose it might work? That it would furnish the clue I seek."

"How can it not but provide such. Let's be about it, Jacob Marley." He reached out his hand and laid it on Jacob's sleeve. Jacob stood and did follow with him.

The mist that had laid white and low before now rose up and around to engulf them in its property. Inside the haze Jacob and Ambroise were able only to see what appeared to be halls and steps, streets and buildings, gates and yards. Ever changing and floating, without color and remaining vague and vaporous until they were in what to Jacob was a familiar place from his youth. At that juncture the fog began to take on a solidity and hue that gave it form and construct.

"You know this place, Jacob?"

"I do. It is my schoolroom when just a boy. But why have you brought me here?"

"Remember, I do not choose what you envision, Jacob. I only manifest what you, in your heart, need to be shown. I am only an usher for what you yourself know you must know. There is something here that you needs recollect . Think upon it, Jacob Marley."

Jacob knew he was a parish boy at this public school for a short time only. Only until discord did rent his family. Then what was it he must see here?

The halls he and Ambroise walked were at recess and ran wild with young boys, acting as if brigands on the high seas. Then looking into one of the rooms along the wall Jacob spied Thomas Glossery among a crowd of older boys. "I do remember him well," Jacob said as he pointed out the youth. "It is my Tommy."

Older and taller than the majority of the students Tommy was almost a man among the smaller brood. Broad of shoulder, thin of thigh, his blond curls tumbled over his ears, his eyes shone bright with confidence. Surrounded by his crowd he leaned confidently back on a chair appraising the smaller boy sitting on a stool in front of him. It was a younger Jacob Marley, then only a child of seven, and ever so earnest in his attendance.

Old Jacob said to Ambroise, "I was his fag, you know, doing his errands and chores for him. It was a position of honor, and proud to be in the position I was. Tommy was the most popular of all the boys, destined for much."

"And why was he important to your quest?"

"He was also the one who perceived and inaugurated me into my stranger nature. He was my first amorist, my intimate. He set me on the path that was, many years down the line, to be my ruination."

"You were his bum-boy then?"

"Aye. Blunt as that seems. But I was not abused by it. I

HE LEANED BACK ON HIS CHAIR APPRAISING THE SMALLER BOY

was grateful for his showing me my true self."

Ambroise turned and looked in the opposite direction. When Jacob too had turned the two were instantly transported to another, later, time.

Months, perhaps fourteen, gone by and there were different circumstance set before them. Jacob was a bit further along, a bit taller, but now very thin, wearing a dismal uniform of grey baize, his feet shod with heavy clogs. He was picking strands of oakum. And he was sorely disturbed.

"You are in difficult circumstance, Jacob. No longer a parish boy, now at the workhouse? How have you fallen so far?"

"A great catastrophe did befall all of us, Ambroise. Father died of the cholera. Mother did sacrifice her legacy to bad investments and she was carried off to the poorhouse at Marblesea. I was separated from her, becoming a Workhouse orphan. Never to be reunited as she did pass from ague not eight months after."

"Truly a series of unfortunate happenstance's. You did manage to escape though. How did that transpire?"

"Through the mechanization's of the beadle on my behalf. Although that was not his purpose he did, in fact, save me." Jacob heaved a great sigh and prepared to explain. "I had become during my stay in that accursed place enamoured of another of my own. A boy younger than myself who sought protection with me from the harsh and unforgiving drudgery. Strange. At this distance I do not even remember his name, but we'd sought solace in each others society. We seldom parted and did uphold each other. The beadle, stumbling on our liaison and fearing our symptoms of sexual sympathy might contaminate all and others did post a bill and offer me for apprenticeship to the highest bidder. It was a way to be rid of me.

But it became, instead, my salvation. For upon the very day I was meant to be shanghaied off to the millworks of Lancashire—where it was rumored children were ground up and mixed with the pussy's to provide filling for baker's pies—I was articled, for his good consideration, to one Mr. Fezziwig, a merchant of imported and domestic goods, then of London and environs.

I was bound indenture, until my majority, in the magisterial presence, and was taken from the workhouse by Fezziwig and installed at Aldersgate Street, north from St Paul's, where his warehouse did reside. In Mr. Fezziwig I was blessed. He was a good and kind master and I did manage to bloom and grow under his tutelage. Until my fifteenth year I was there alone and content to be so. Six years in is when a new apprentice did appear to disrupt and affect my entire existence."

The fog surrounding Old Jacob and Ambroise became dark and dirty as the streets of London town did grow and appear to them. A store front with ill lit windows shining through the murk drew them inside the same ramshackle building. "And there he is!", Jacob exclaimed. "Old Fezziwig."

The object of Jacob's attention was bent over his books and diligently at his task. A portly middle-aged man in a Welsh wig he showed a kindly disposition and was always able to smile at the bustle that went on all around him. He sat at his high stool and looked out on a posted area where the clerk, a gangly young Jacob in linen shirt, high stock with cravat, long tights and boots, did bend also over his individual assignment. Beyond the office area was a large warehouse engaged in other manufacture and function. Men hustled with sacks, climbed ladders with boxes, and generally contributed to the din and industry of the place.

Old Jacob, standing beside Ambroise, felt his heart go faster at the next event he did witness. For coming in the door from outside was a gentlemen with a young lad. Mr. Fezziwig climbed down from his stool and went to greet them, clapping the gentleman on the shoulder while beckoning Jacob to come forth.

"Jacob," he said in his usual jovial manner, "This here is

our latest apprentice, young Ebenezer Scrooge. Our wizard of the accounts, Mr. Marley." He smiled as he introduced the two. The lad stepped forward and held out his hand, "Your servant, Mr. Marley." he said in a tone so very grave for one so young it caused Old Marley to chuckle at the memory.

Fezziwig went on. "Jacob, take Ebenezer under your protection and show him the means of his position."

It came to young Jacob at that shining moment that his search was over, he had happened upon his twin. In this young lad, still with down on his cheek, Jacob finally knew his soul's desire. He felt for this boy an incomprehensible attraction, aroused not only by his form and features, but by his intellect and friendship. They were, he was sure, from that moment to find their lives entwined the same as the honeysuckle and the brier rose.

Jacob took the lad to his quarters and helped stow his few processions. "No doubt you feel new and strange in this, Mr. Scrooge?, he said.

"Some." Ebenezer replied.

"Do you not find society the same? I feel we are on the edge of great change. That a new abidance and social purity will prevail. Do you agree?"

Ebenezer stood and again looked grave. "I think the world a savage and brazen place. One must fortify oneself against it. Protect and guard against its hardships."

"I dare say we have much in common, Mr. Scrooge."

"I hope so, Mr. Marley."

Jacob was bound then to make it so.

Ambroise spoke. "You did tether your heart to Ebenezer Scrooge that day?"

Jacob answered, "Aye. But I knew also that I must keep it veiled and hidden. That if my true nature be known to him it would break our budding acquaintance. I would then lose him, and I could not chance that. So I closed the fountains of my heart and nipped that bud that sought light and warmth."

Now scene after scene of their togetherness flashed before Jacob. Scrooge and Marley on the Strand. Spending a day together at the Vic. Laughing at the pantomime. Having deep meaningful conversation at the ale house. As they grew they became close as siblings, close as Achilles and Patroclus did in their time.

"You found much in each other, Jacob."

"We did. But always I was careful not to cross that line. I must find that more base satisfaction on personal excursions to Fleet St. and the West End, or in the private salons on Dexter Street. Which I did, and found ready acquaintance with many of my own nature. And I could be sure to always find one who resembled Ebenezer, for it satisfied a part that could not with the bona fide person."

"And Ebenezer himself. Did he find like solace?"

Instantly before Jacob and Ambroise was laid a new tableau. Old Jacob watched as Ebenezer found, at Fezziwig's Christmas fete, a like minded girl by the name of Belle. He watched as they danced every reel together, finding much in themselves to admire. Each longing look between then was like a dagger in Jacobs breast. He was at pains to cover his distress at this new attraction.

"So, Ebenezer did fall in love?"

"Yes. While I had to stand aside and espy this happening. It was a heartache. She was a comely lass I did admit, but she was without prospects and was unsuitable as a companion."

"Is that your actual thought or is there some other more sinister underlying reason, Jacob."

"I wish to see no more. Can we move on, Ambroise?"

The hourglass turned another turn and Jacob saw himself, now suffering the constant strain of concealment. "I feared losing my reputation and my dearest friend. I knew the incompatibility of my religious belief and my bodily appetite. If widely known there would certainly have been social isolation and worse. It was a fearful burden."

HAVING DEEP MEANINGFUL CONVERSATION

Jacob Marley

Ambroise tilted his head in sympathy. "I do appreciate your position, good fellow. Grievously, over time it made you unkind and snappish to many, did it not?"

Jacob nodded sadly. "I was a derisive and wily cur for many."

"You did wound and distress those who might have, however unknowingly, compromised your narrow circle. Look at what now transpires." Ambroise held out his hand to direct Old Jacob's vision.

A much younger Jacob and a fair Belle together come around a corner, their heads leaned together in earnest conversation. "My dear girl," Jacob says, "I do but advise you of the commonplace. It is well known to all who have congress with him. He has, I foreswear, found another. Another golden mistress to obey. Money has replaced you, my dear. And in that you have a worthy opponent, I'll wager."

"But we are long betrothed. I cannot see him turning from me."

"Wealth and the seeking thereof are a strong and ever flickering flame for most men. Think you the power to pull Ebenezer from that alter ?"

"I must find out. I need to challenge the profit and know where I stand?" She hesitated and turned to Jacob with an inquiry. "Shouldn't I? You know him better than most, Mr. Marley. Will I win in this?"

"I know not. He is very like a moth in this regard. But I bid you try."

"And I shall."

Belle turned from Jacob and went inside the offices where Scrooge did hold court. Jacob stayed where he was and looked on them from his vantage at the facing window.

"And behold your face, Jacob." Ambroise said to Old Jacob. "I see only cunning. And slippery manipulation. Scheming, rapacious, and triumphant. Did it occur to you that her gentle touch was needed to stay Ebenezer from the course he did travel? Or did you only have thought of what you craved? You sought only the removal of a rival for his affection."

"It is enough, Ambroise. Show me no more."

"But there is more to see. We do run another column."

The mist roiled and swept before them and then formed into the front of a small housing block. The two men stood together on the street. Scrooge was handing Jacob a card and saying in earnest, "Go quickly, dear friend, and seek out the apothecary. Fan is in dire need. I will stay and watch over her. Please hurry, Jacob."

Old Jacob watched his younger self take leave and head for the nearest street with the appropriate commerce. When the young Jacob found the proper stall he entered intending to ask for the assistance his companion's sister dearly required. But as offen happens in the course of young mens lives, fate had other plans for Jacob Marley that day.

The apothecary he sought turned out to be a comely male of fair youth and great beauty. Jacob was drawn to him and in like manner he to Jacob. Thinking not of his errand and knowing only the needs of his body, Jacob and the man did tarry in a back room of the stall and share their fleshen poles, exploring their mutual necessity to the extent of an extra two quarters of an hour. After achieving conquest, remembering his charge, Jacob sent the druggist on to his patient.

"Would Fan have lived had he arrived earlier, Ambroise?"

"I cannot reply. What happened won't be altered. These are but shadows of the event. They are what they are. But Scrooge did take this greatly. The black band he wore took him another step on the path to his flint like heart."

"And I was the cause was I not?"

"And you too took another step toward putting yourself in Scrooge's way. You wanted him only for yourself, didn't you Jacob? You did dote on him and seek a spiritual love beyond his comprehension. To hold his beloved form in your embrace, to make him your single object, your gallant, your infatuate."

A YOUNGER JACOB AND A FAIR BELLE

THE APOTHECARY WAS A COMELY MALE OF FAIR YOUTH AND BEAUTY

Jacob Marley

The mist again rose and now scenes did run swiftly past. Years went by in moments, days did pass, and age did come upon the faces of the participants. Jacob saw himself at thirty, thirty-five, forty, forty-one, two, three. It showed him grown prosperous from business and fat with the greed that accompanies that goal. It also showed him wandering through the back streets of London in search of a companionship his desire for Scrooge would not fulfill. The parade did finally slow and stop at the age of forty-five.

"Oh, no, Ambroise. I won't see this."

"But you must." Ambroise put his hand on Jacob's shoulder and held him in place.

The fog settled and formed a street in the Seven Dials district. A low, grubby, forbidding street of straggling houses, ill-proportioned and deformed by neglect and age. A place where disputes ended in blows, idle men leaned against lampposts, and half-naked children wallowed in the gutters. Jacob appeared and did make haste to his goal. The staircase of one of the tenements, perhaps more disreputable than any of the others.

"I knew I was out of my place but the lad had entreated me so strongly I gave in to his pleading."

"A lad?", Ambroise enquired.

"A lad. Ernest Thackery by name. A fellow sufferer I had become much attached to. An incomprehensible attraction to be sure. We were of vastly different classes. Him a rent-boy I had discovered one night at the music hall in Clement's Lane and become besotted about. It did pass human understanding to be sure, but so it was. He was a fair and pretty boy and I did find sustenance in him. I had hope I might assist him in rising above his station, that we might walk together."

Jacob knocked on the door of the garret and it opened. Ernest stood there with his sunny smile alighting Jacob's heart at its brilliance. He was dressed in his meager finest, tight trousers, an ill-fitting jacket, with a collar too big and stained from meals past, wrapped with a limp cravat. He bid Jacob enter and nervously stood aside.

Inside Jacob found a bed, a pitiful little trunk, shabby trousers and a jacket hung on nails pounded into the wall. Under them was a dirty table with a candle-end flickering in a tarnished stand. Next to it a tiny seasonal tree made of feathers wound round a dowel, bits of foil and wool applied as ornament. On the mantle stood a looking-glass in a rosewood frame and a crystal mug, won in a lottery perhaps, or a gift from a client—these made the only decoration in the room.

"I'm so glad you came," Ernest said.

"Was it important that I appear here, lad? I could have easily rented a hotel elsewhere for us."

"It might have better suited your sensibilities, I'm sure, but I have need to speak with you, Mr. Marley. There is a proposition I need to make, and here is where I am most comfortable."

"A proposition? What is it you wish to ask, Ernest? Be quick about it. And clear."

Ernest bid him sit and then said, "Our acquaintance has been of great pleasure to me, Mr. Marley, it has indeed. But it has rewarded me little. I wish it weren't like this, but I'm in need of alms. I'm wanting your purchase of these..." Ernest pulled from a box sitting on the table a packet of two letters tied with a grimy ribbon of blue. "I have held on to these for such an occasion as this. You do write a fine and effusive note, Mr. Marley. They did gladden my heart at their sentiment. I would be much vexed if they were to show up at an auction room. Would you not also?"

Jacob reached for the packet but Ernest pulled it away. Jacob knew this boy had him for blackmail. It was a constant threat to men of his station. Jacob knew of others of his kind who had fallen into this same trap. He resigned himself to the mechanization's of this foul boy. "And what is this amount you have need of?"

"I'm wanting a years allowance. Three hundred would be

"I'M WANTING YOUR PURCHASE OF THESE..."

enough, I think. Or I will pawn them." Ernest smiled again, but its former brightness was now shaded with wicked malice.

"And you would never need more, boy? The letters would be mine again?"

"Oh, for sure, Mr. Marley. These would be in your own procession upon your departure this very night."

"And the others. I have writ you more than this, much to my regret and chagrin."

'Those I would find useful on another occasion."

Jacob stood then his ire colouring his face an angry crimson. "I can not allow that." He reached again for the packet and sought to grab it from Ernest

Ernest stepped away backing up against the table that stood beside him. This rattled the table causing the lit candle to loose from its stand. It fell upon the cotten wool wraped at the base of the feather tree he had used as a sign of the season. It did catch aflame, which quickily consumed the tree. The flame grew and in turn jumped to the hanging clothes that lined the wall. Now they too were alight. Ernest tried heartily to suffocate the fire, beating at it with his hands. Instead the blaze jumped again, this time catching the starched linen of his collar. He yelled and slapped at his burning face with his hands. Jacob, in horror, did shrink from the scene. He ran from the conflagration, down the stairs to the dark of the street, where he stopped.

Old Jacob, seeing this, had turned away from the sight. "Bend you back and see, Jacob.", Ambrose instructed. "You were attentive then were you not?"

First the room and soon the building caught afire. Jacob stood there watching as it burned finally to the ground. "You took heed as that boy did shriek and agonize. Then you turned and walked away, knowing that the boy was finished. Did you feel no pity for his circumstance."

"But, Ambroise, I did feel ponderous guilt on this. What was I to do? I could not let the vile boy achieve his aim. He would have continued to bleed me."

"You could have assisted him, Jacob. You could have done your part in preventing the destruction. But you did not. This was most grievous on your part, Jacob Marley, and you should have received the punishment you merited."

"Do I not now suffer from this?" Jacob held up the chains that wound around him, cosseting his movements, weighing upon him greatly. "Is this not my punishment for my sins? Have I not paid for them threefold in these last seven years? How much more am I to endure?" He wailed a bloodcurdling scream that rent the fog and caused the previous scene to disappear in the mizzle of time.

The vapors quickly flew forward six more years, reformed, and showed, in that instant, Jacob's bed chamber.

Jacob lay outstretched and dying on his bed. Ebenezer Scrooge leaned over him, hearing, but not understanding, Jacob's importuning and warnings. Ebanezer would not heed his vision of the afterlife.

"No, Ambroise, why am I to view this. To suffer his disdain, his lack of caring upon my departure? Ambroise, this is too cruel."

"Watch and learn, Jacob. There is something you need to know. in this."

Jacob reluctantly did watch as Scrooge pennied his eyes and covered his corpse with linen. Scrooge turned and left the chamber, retiring to his own apartments across the hall.

Once there, and away from undertakers eyes, he slumped into his chair and began to sob. "Oh, Jacob," he cried. "My much loved friend. Dead. Dead! Disenthralled of flesh and risen to His arms. I am grievously saddened that one so good, so kind, so loving, so honest and dear should be taken from me. Time will not soften this until the grave closes over remembrance, and we are reunited." Scrooge continued to cry his anguish, his sorrow.

Jacob said to Ambroise. "I knew not that he was so regretfully affected."

YOU TURNED AND WALKED AWAY

Jacob Marley

"He was, and wore the black bandage in memory for a good six months, as if you were a brother. He even had the bells of St. Martin's-in-the-Field peal nine and fifty-one for you. And it cost him dear, it did. You think he did not care?"

"I did not know. I did not know."

The vapor again rose up around them and when it cleared Jacob and Ambroise had returned to where they had begun. The white place of infinite area and aspect.

"Our sojourn is complete, Jacob. You have seen all that you needed to. I bid you wait here for your next guide."

Passage III

And Jacob did wait. A quarter hour, then at the half, and then again the quarter and ten more. He stood in that vacant and colorless place and worried to himself who or what he had caused to call on Ebenezer Scrooge. What strange spirit had he occasioned to appear to him? Was it some fearful and horrible wailing specter? Or a more benevolent and kinder fairy? Jacob feared for himself as he now must also meet this very same ghost.

He then questioned what it was he must be shown. This second spirit was called Present. Did not Jacob know all too well his current predicament? His own present. Was he not burdened with it all the waking hours and days of his tortured existence? Was it not tied so heavily to his very soul? What Present was he to witness? Must he see more of the sad lot he must continually trod each passing day? Or perhaps he was to be shown another more favorful and contented aspect?

He felt a large and heavy hand come round from his back and land upon his shoulder. A voice colored with age and fatigue said, "I have arrived, Jacob Marley. Are you ready?"

Jacob turned and looking on the personage standing then before him did feel great relief. "Ah, good Spirit," for before him was a treasured friend of earlier acquaintance. "You have come as the second usher? And glad of it I shall be." For this specter, like Jacob himself, had trod the same paths as he, entreating and wailing upon the Earth. In this they had supported each other. But Jacob had not seen him of late and wondered at his absence, and did also perceive a change in him from previous times.

"I am, Jacob. I have lately been made the specter of the here and now. Present and at hand. But my time is short and we must not tarry."

"I can see, old companion." For the ghost did indeed appear before him now aged and weary. Dull grey streaked his hair and beard where once it was brown and shining. His eyes were covered with membranes that clouded and dimmed his vision. Under them folds of sagging skin lined his face with time. His voice rattled with lassitude where once it was hardy and jocular. "I beg you not fret, old friend. For I will soon return to you robust and well before a fortnight has passed. Upon the New Year I shall be renewed." And Jacob did relax his apprehensions. "Now, take hold of my robe and come with me."

Jacob did as he was instructed, touching Spirits fur lined sleeve. They both together went up on the air beneath them and slid across the space, where they did approach a door. As they arrived it opened of its own accord, not needing the touch of either of their hands to do so. They slipped through the entrance way and into the darkness beyond.

As it slammed shut behind them Jacob found himself in the exact same rooms he had himself visited earlier that evening. He was standing then in Scrooge's own chambers. What was not the same for him was the amount of light that streamed in through the window that had not been drawn. It was still early evening and Ebenezer had not yet arrived from his meager dinner. Jacob's visit would not happen until later.

The phantom, with a withered and shaking finger, pointed him toward that same window. Jacob looked down and out on the courtyard that provided access to Scrooge's apartments.

Ebenezer, huddled against the quickly darkening night, was just then approaching his front door. He reached for the knob and then stepped back. There was a look of fear and astoundment coloring his face. His arm went up and his hand pointed to the door. He was seeing Jacob's face superimposed on his knocker.

Jacob, resting above him at the window, did chuckle at his reaction. "I got his attention there, did I not? He was made to be much wary."

Scrooge next came through the door, up the stairs, and into his chamber. He threw the locks tight, and once feeling secure, went for his dressing room. Jacob and the wraith followed behind him and observed as he readied for the night. After slipping into his gown and robe he stepped to a small cabinet hanging next to his wardrobe. Opening it he laid his forehead on the edge, looked inside and said, "Ah, Jacob, another day has gone..."

Jacob started and said to the ghost, "What ho?"

Spirit answered, "It is a ritual performed each and every evening for these past seven years. He is steadfast in it."

"No, I did hear mine own name. I must see what this is about."

Jacob rose, as haunts are want to do, and floated over to hover just above Ebenezer's shoulder so as to get a better view. He did see a collection of objects set carefully inside the finely wrought box. One was a medium sized plaster painted oval. "Why, I recollect that. It is the silhouette I commissioned on a trip Ebenezer and I took to Brighton for the waters years ago. I thought it missing. And there is my watch, with its fob and seal still attached. And a pair of my buckskin gloves laid carefully beside a hank of hair tied in a Gordian knot."

"A shrine of remembrance," Spirit said.

Ebenezer finished, "I am another day closer to our reunion, dearest friend." He lovingly touched upon each object and then carefully closed the box. Upon locking it he retired to his fire and bowl of gruel.

Jacob shook his head. "I am dumfounded. Most assuredly. I knew him not to be so devoted. Nor so tender."

"He was a friend to be sure."

"More than I knew."

Time slipped forward and Scrooge lay upon his bed in an agitated and restless sleep. He tossed and flipped and kicked and moaned. "You spirits did visit and invade his dreams, and cause him much fretfulness it would appear. Was there a result of your actions upon him?"

Spirit again pointed to the window. "Look upon this and judge for yourself." Jacob could see that outside it had now become bright with morning light. Beams shone through the glass and did break and shadow on the floor. Dust danced and flew in its bright stream. Also dancing was a joyous Ebenezer who did skip and gambol in his rooms and delight in the action of it. "I am saved!" he cried, his arms waving above his head. He started as a mirror caught his jig. He leaned in and, observing his own happiness, called himself a humbug, then laughed at his doing it.

When Ebenezer's maid-of-all-work brought his morning tea, Old Jacob was delighted that Scrooge, with his good humor, sorely affrighted her and then rewarded her with a guinea for a gift on Christmas day.

The ghost and Jacob were well-pleased also as Scrooge beckoned to a youngster below and sent him off to purchase a large fowl. Ebenezer quickly dressed and then met the boy and the poulterer at the front door not more than a half hour later.

Ebenezer took the boy and his sled and going from store to stall piled it high with fruits and nuts, tea and coffee, vegetables and condiments, toys and fillabows so the sled reminded Scrooge of the throne the spirit had sat upon on their first meeting just hours before. And on his lips were a Happy Christmas for all. Coins did spew from his purse in torrents of gratitude and benevolence. He knew he was making up for many past omissions and did in haste pass it on.

Jacob and the Spirit followed the pair with their sled as they made their way to the suburbs and a poor street in Camden Town. The home of his clerk Bob Cratchit. They watched as Scrooge left the overflowing sled at the door, knocked, and retired to a hidden corner where he could see the expression of shock and delight on the face of Bob, Mrs. Cratchit, and all the assorted Cratchits.

In a twinkling Scrooge was in a finer neighborhood and knocking on the door of his nephew, Fred. Once opened by a maid servant he did put his fingers to his lips and bid her not announce him. Instead he slid open the doors to the parlor and waited until Fred saw him standing there in his newly acquired attitude of humility. "Would you welcome your Uncle, Fred?" he softly inquired.

"Would I? By my leave, sir, I am delighted. Look here, dear, it is Uncle Scrooge!", and to the cheers of the gathering old Scrooge was welcomed into the bosom of his small family.

At a later point in their merriment the parlor door was again slid open and a serving woman did enter with a small bundle cradled in her arms.

"Come here, Uncle," Fred called. "And greet your grand-niece. She is only a bit of a thing still, but will be a pleasure to her Father and Mother in years to come." Scrooge leaned over to stare at the cherubic face of the next generation before him. Fred again spoke. "We have named her Fan, in honour of my dear Mother."

"And my sister," Scrooge said as a tear wet his eye. Then he looked up and into the face of the nursery maid, a woman of his own age serving in this capacity. He started, looked again and said, "Upon my word, I know you. Is it Belle?"

"That is my name, good sir. How you come by it."

"I am your old acquaintance, Ebenezer Scrooge. Do you recollect me?"

"Aye I do, though it has been many years."

She returned the child to its crib and then, sitting together in the upper hallway, did have discourse with Scrooge. She told him of her great loss a few years before. Of the disease that took her husband and children all at once, leaving her in reduced circumstance. As a safeguard against want she had returned to service as a governess and had been most content at the call of this fine family.

Scrooge, in his new found happiness, assured her that he would guarantee that her circumstance would remain solvent and service to his nephew and grand-niece would be a choice not a chore. Then he asked if he could return and pay court even at this advanced time in his life. She was amenable and did smile at the idea of it. As did old Scrooge seeing again the possibility of companionship in his future.

Still hovering above them Old Jacob turned to his kindly guide and asked, "And will this sense of generous benevolence continue, Spirit? Will Ebenezer take to heart the lessons you have showed him? Will he remain changed for the better?"

Jacob Marley

"Do not fear, Jacob. Our work and your intercession have achieved their ends. It will always be said of old Scrooge that he kept Christmas well, if any man alive possessed the knowledge."

And Jacob did feel gladness and joy in his heart in this, for his dearest friend had been saved from his fate.

"But there is one more place for you see, Jacob Marley." Grabbing Jacob's sleeve Spirit did skid away from the scene of Scrooge and the possibility of love, and hurry with him toward an unknown destination. They went flying through streets and alleys causing snow to whirl in sparkling drifts behind them. When at last they did slow the ghost and his charge were left on the steps leading into St. Steven's Hospital, a dingy and festering institution much feared by the souls who had need of it. Many who went in never reappeared from it bowels.

"Why do you bring me here, kind Spirit?" Jacob asked. "This place is where the weak seek solace, the contagious are isolated, and the poor come to die. What is there here for me? I am already dead and far beyond solace."

"You are to enter and seek out the ward. That is all I have been told."

"But I dread what I might see."

"It is for your benefit, Jacob, trust us in that."

"Will you accompany me?"

"Not this time, Jacob. I am too old and infirm to make the journey." And indeed it was so, for in the short time they had been in company the apparition had continued to age. He now was white haired and bearded, bent over, and needing support to stay upright. An ancient, who would make even Methuselah look a right elf. "Now go, friend, before our time must expire."

Jacob rose and did glide up to the door, which again opened without aid and allowed him entrance. Jacob rode through the darkened halls and then onward again, knowing not where he would stop. He passed offices and cubicles, clinics and examination rooms until finally he arrived at a large chamber crammed row upon row with hard wooden pallets. Upon these uncomfortable benches laid personages in various stages of illness and suffering. Their moans and cries did rent the air and cause a terrible din. What a pestilent box this was Jacob thought upon the sight of it. Jacob was dragged again forward into the room until he hung suspended in front of a bed holding a sickly man in the throes of a fever. Beside the sick man sat the watchwoman. A woman processed of what did appear to be a caring disposition as she had hold of the patients hand and did speak soothingly to him. As she ministered her inadequate remedy the man did flail at unseen torments before him, moaning at their slaps on him, trying unsuccessfully to push them away.

Soon another woman did arrive to relieve the first. She bent over the patient and bid him drink from the vile she proffered upon him. In a whisper to her companion she said, "This laudanum should calm him for now. Unfortunate soul, he is not long is he?"

The second woman nodded in agreement. "Poor Mr. Thackery, the putrid fever has him I'm afraid."

"Aye, the typhus will prove fatal for him before this night's over, I'm sure. Has his delirium lessened any?"

"No, he does still rave. He slaps at his head to extinguish flames that were put out long ago, as the scars on his cheek attest to. A shame it is, when young he must have been a pretty one."

Jacob hearing this put the pieces together and realized that the man lying before him was none other than that Ernest Thackery, his one time blackmailer, and one he had until then felt sure was long gone. Was it possible the vile lad had escaped the building fire and now instead faced his Maker from disease and affliction? Could it be?

Jacob leaned over to get a closer look at this cadaverous creature. Although older and raced with fever it surely could

BESIDE THE SICK MAN SAT THE WATCHWOMAN

have been him. The features, even with the scaring on his cheek, were that familiar. Good God, then the rent-boy had lived! Jacob was not responsible for the death of that boy, now a man, lying here at last receiving his just desserts.

This realization brought Jacob upright with shock and he did back away from the body. He looked upon the man with staggering amazement. He finally knew for a certainty he had carried his culpability in this counterfeit misdeed for naught. He was innocent in its reason. He himself at last was free from blame. Jacob felt a longheld weight lifted off him. He received peace in this at last.

Jacob prepared to leave the ward, thinking he had accomplished his reason in this, but he did not. He stayed floating above the ward and observing, for those who directed and controlled his journey decided there was still more for him to see in this infectious place. Prior to this moment Jacob had been only attentive to his discovery of Ernest Thackery, but now he became aware of the greater vault surrounding him. He saw before him spirits. Many spirits, all standing beside and looking down on their now decomposing corporeal forms. These spirits were fresh and therefore most confused and wondering of their situation. Many had not yet realized they had passed on and were just becoming cognizant at that intelligence. They moaned at their fate, and gnawed and rent their breasts. This was a terrible crying sound, indeed, and did continue until before them their next act was revealed.

Soon after their essence had vacated their bodies they each were bathed in a light. White for some, blue for others, and for still others a black that was night personified. This light was somehow able to give both peace and instruction to these newly formed souls.

Those in the white light would turn and find before them a set of steps leading up into a vast and comforting brilliance. With beatific smiles on their faces they would climb toward another plain. A different existence.

Jacob Marley

Those in the blue light were soon directed in another direction. Beyond the side of the room they gathered to await the application of their fetters so they would go forward and atone for the transgressions they performed in their last lifespan. Jacob knew this route all to well.

Those standing in the dark light would also turn and they did find at their feet a gapping hole leading them down into a vast inky shadow. A look of great sadness accompanied their decent into the abyss that awaited them. Once there they also went to a another heath to find their fates.

This all went on without incident and with great solemnity, each soul passing without sorrow or comment. Then Ernest Thackery, who had just moments before passed and found his end, stepped up. The gapping dark hole awaited him and he did recoil at it. He turned and in attempting escape fell to the floor and scrambled on hands and knees away from the edge, loudly protesting at his ill-omened end. The darkness he was meant to descend into began to whirl and then to spin, making a dreadful loud whooshing sound as it did. The sinkhole soon became alive and writhed and squirmed and developed into a nest of wriggling eels like those found at a fishmonger shop in Billingsgate, great black serpents hissing and darting from their pit at Ernest crawling away in despair. His fear further causing him to cower and cringe, he scooted on his haunches away from this otherworldly lot of vipers now more frighted than before. The eels did begin to twist on each other and in this they did lengthen and stretch, then slither from the pit toward Ernest. The horror upon his face intensified and he screamed as the slithery black dragons wound round his leg and began to pull him irrevocability toward the maw lying before him. He yelled and pleaded and soon disappeared into the gloom and damnation of that dark place, while the various other spirits did not deign to take notice of the ruckus. They just walked in their stupor onward to their fates.

Jacob, in a moment of pity for his erstwhile bleeder and

HIS LAST GHOST HAD ARRIVED

Jacob Marley

extorter, had turned away. When he turned back he found himself once again outside the hospital where Spirit had before bid him go in. But that Spirit was not there anymore. Jacob was alone on the street. He searched and knew not where he was next to wander.

As the city clock tolled the hour he felt a cold and frosty breeze lite upon his back. Turning toward it he saw a heavily cloaked black figure standing in the distance. And so he knew. His last ghost had arrived.

Passage IV

Jacob stood in front of the spirit and waited. For several minutes he stayed there. The ghost spoke not at all. He waited more and the apparition continued to remain mute. When he could take the silence no more Jacob spoke. "You are the third of my visitors, are you not?"

He received no response. Hesitant, Jacob went on, "The last spirit was of seasons present. Then am I standing before the ghost of events yet to come?" Again there was no answer. "What is it you would show me? For I know my future. I am to continue on the path currently set before me, is that not so?" Then a dim hope lighted a flame in his bosom. "Or do you offer a chance at reprieve from this dismal end I have for so long endured? Please, benevolent specter, if there be a hope of this show me the way."

The specter, continuing his silence, raised his arm and turned, bidding Jacob to go in the direction he indicated.

"I am to follow? But to what destination? Is this the way to the hope I prophesized?" The ghost simply stayed in the attitude he had taken. "All right, Spirit, I will comply. But I must admit much trepidation at this request."

Jacob then moved in the direction he was bid to attend. He continued on that path for several leagues, going onward with only swirling fog and no markers to guide him. His senses numbed by the mist he stopped, incredulous, when he saw rising before him a set of great ponderous doors.

These two doors were standing many measures tall, so tall that Jacob could only just make out the tops when looking up. Fashioned of a dark impenetrable wood, their moldings were ornately carved with garlands and blooms. The doorknob was as large as a child's head with an escutcheon the size of a grown woman, the keyhole large enough for a terrier to crawl through.

It did, in just its implacability, alight much dread in Jacob. "What are these doors entrance too?" he asked. "Is this an approach or a culmination. Spirit, tell me. Where or what does this lead to? Speak, damn you, do not keep me incognitant in this. I must know!"

The spirit only stayed its place and again raised his arm. At this the doors, with a mighty creak and groan, began to slowly open. Jacob, when an opening large enough for him to slip through appeared, carefully stepped forward into what he could now see to be a chamber beyond.

Inside Jacob was confronted by a massive stone built cloister having boundless sweeping arches overhead and going on ahead of him by not much short of an acres length. The floor was made of black and white squares, each the height of a man and styled in a repeated diamond. On each side were built enclosed bleachers. In these sat, in orderly rows, the shades and shadows of humanity long gone. Spooks and goblins, manes and wraiths, banshees and eidolon all sat attentively, their death masks facing to the front of this vast expanse.

Many yards ahead of Jacob stood a lone ghost. This former man stood alone in a circle of light shining bright in the gloomy atmosphere that prevailed. This light caused him to be the main focus of the ghostly spectators attention. Standing with his head bowed, Jacob could see the chains this man wore about his waist, as did Jacob his own, were longer and more heavily wrought than his and lay around his legs in a pool so dense as to obscure his feet from view.

Jacob, by then, was made fully aware he had stepped into a judges chamber, a tribunal, a judicatory of some last resort. A Spirits Bench, if you will, higher in status than even the Court of Delegates at the Doctor's Commons. A place for those caught in their accursed circumstance to plead their case.

The ghost now standing inquiry was in front of an immense towering bench raising up before him. As tall as the doors Jacob had lately entered, and perhaps a bit more, it rose up to shadow the plaintiff in its majesty. At the ground stood the plaintiffs prosecutor. Swathed in great draped robes and white wig he was also spirit, made of decomposing flesh and rotting bone, his fleshless fingers holding papers which he shuffled as if playing a hand of whist.

To the right, looking balefully upon the court, sat a jury of peers. Twelve specters in line, each in various stages of decay, each malignant in their aspect, each charged with deciding the poor souls fate who stood currently before them.

Reigning over the prosecutor, attached onto the bench, was a heraldic shield upon which was carved the courts blazon of arms, an upright horse rampant being devoured by a pack of mongrel curs, and above that a motto—*Mort finem respice.* Death consider the end.

And above this device sat the chief magistrate himself. He looked from his perch with a nocuous and pestilential mien as he wore the black and scarlet of his rank with a long wig of goat hair dressed in rolls to his shoulder. His eyes were red rimmed and piercing. The cheeks were sunken and pocked. There was a nose bulbous with too much drink, and a hairy mole sat beside a downturned deeply crevassed mouth that seemed to perpetually move over toothless gums. This was situated above a wiry chin set on a turkey waddle of a neck. His hands were freckled and veined finished with bony accusing fingers. In them he held a long wooden hearing horn held always to his ear. Deaf as a doorpost in one ear and only a tiny ability in the other he would lean forward to make himself closer to a sound.

The solicitor below, now standing, held out a page and read from it. His voice ringing loudly for the judge far above him it echoed off and bounced round the court chamber. "Having heard your testimony and considering its merit how does the jury find this petitioner? Your verdict, my blighted sirs?" One by one the ghostly jurors held their hands out flat and then turned their thumbs in a downward fashion. As each and every one of the twelve condemned their charge sorrowful moans from the spectators rent the air . "Having received said verdict what justice will you hand down, your worship?"

The judge laid down his ear horn and held his arms above his head and through some unknown magic between his hands did appear a black square of cloth. This he brought to his head and laid it so one corner hung down on his forehead .

In a voice high pitched and as dry and stale as three day

THE SOLICITOR HELD OUT A PAGE AND READ

old bread, he shrilled, "By sovereignty and prerogative I find you blamable in this instant. Transgressor, you are sentenced to an additional try at finding your answer. And, with God's mercy, this time you do find your Elysium." He pointed at the man. "Be gone now and seek your purpose."

The accused, standing on a black square, looked down and watched horrified as the floor under him dissolved and disappeared from under his feet. Finally, with a terrified shriek, he fell to his fate, his scream diminishing as he sank deeper into the chasm below him.

The prosecutor then stood again, "Jacob Marley to the dock," he called. "Come forward and plead for your immortal soul."

The judge leaned over his bench with his horn to his ear. "What's that? What say you? Speak up."

The gentleman solicitor shouted back, "I called for Marley to appear, my lord."

"Well, why didn't you say so? Louder, my lad, louder."

He sighed at this repeated request. "Yes, your worship." Then he sat again and opened a sheave of papers and began reading.

The dark spirit standing beside Jacob moved his arm in a gesture directing him to go before the bench. Jacob said to him, "Spirit, I am ill prepared for this. I have had no counsel, no aid in this case. How am I to go forward?" The spirit remained in the same position without making comment. "Then I must obey? I needs go to this inquest regardless of my circumstance?" "

The prosecutor again called, this time sharply. "Jacob Marley, find yourself before this tribunal now or suffer the consequences!"

"What? What's that?" the judge asked.

"Marley, sir." he shouted back. "He is yet to appear."

"Where is he then? Don't make our court wait or there will be contempt charges levied."

Jacob went hesitantly forward and stood at the bench, his mind running amok with questions and no answers as he awaited the next development in this bizarre trial.

The judge looked on Jacob with a jaundiced eye. "What's this? Who stands there?"

The solicitor yelled, "I believe this to be Marley, sir."

"Why didn't ye say so. About time, I swear. Go on then, ask your questions. Don't keep the court waiting in this." He slouched back in his chair with the horn to his ear still. "Get on with it, man." he groused.

The prosecutor began the proceedings in a tired and languorous voice. "Hear ye, hear ye, all you having business before this court now attend..."

"You have the voice of a titmouse," the judge shouted. "You must..."

"Yes, my lord," he said louder. He stopped then and rose up to his full height, with pique coloring his face a devils red, he pointed a bony finger at Jacob, and speaking in a tone dripping with a scorpions venom, hissed, 'You, sir, are a degenerate, a pervert, a bugger, a molly, a pederast. I fear that we find ourselves on the cusp of an age of voluptuousness and recklessness. This wickedness you practice hovers over our society as an indecent scarecrow. It is a social scourge and you, sir, were a steady practitioner of this abominable vice, were you not?"

The judge leaned back in his chair. "That's more like it, my boy. That I could hear."

Jacob, shocked and distressed by the prosecutors foul accusations stammered a reply, "How come you by this assumption?"

He looked down with great scorn at Jacob. "True, you have not the look of these ambivalent creatures. I hear not the shrill voice, see not the weak muscles or soft flaccid flesh associated with them. Nor the womanly hips or rouged cheeks, but your disguise does not fool me." He turned and looked up at the judge. "The record is explicit. your worship. He is a

Jacob Marley

Sodomite, this Jacob Marley, and therefore, my lord, his current punishment need not be exchanged." He sat and crossed his arms across his chest.

Jacob, described by many as having no bowels, which was taken to mean they found him "soft" in manner and attitude, somehow, in this instance, found the intestinal fortitude to stand and face his accuser. He took a breath and began, "I suppose I must accept this description of me, sir, but I do strongly dispute and reject your conclusion." There was a gasp from the assembled court. The judge leaned forward. "What? What was that?"

"Why," Jacob pleaded with the judge in a louder voice, "should I be punished for being as I was created by the Master himself? Is not a bee always a bee and will sting because it is his nature? I am as He made me. No less. No more."

The prosecutor shouted at him. "The chains you have carried these past seven seasons say different, sir. They attest to the venality of your past existence, do they not?"

"Your honor, I have these past hours reviewed my history and would surmise from the journey that I did indeed create these fetters I wear. But, may I propose that it was the teachings of that society I was part of that enabled me to pound out and forge them. As long as I spoke only to other peoples disapproval, as long as I only apologized for them, how could I not learn to censure and abhor myself? I could not judge that world fairly? As the lives we led were an enigma to them, so were they to us. To make that society understand was futile. They saw us as lowly actors or specimens to be pinned to a cloth like moths. How could one exist in such conditions? How could it not affect our most intimate feelings?"

The prosecutor pounded one hand against the other. "There are laws and strictures against this practice." He pointed at Jacob again. "You did flaunt and ignore them, did you not?"

"To act as I was dictated, to love as I knew I must, to be the person I needed to be, did force me to find a way in that hostile and restrictive world. I was restrained by a bible backed tyrant of a society who hid behind their masks of righteousness. And, trust me, good sir, there is no mask so evil as that of society's strictures. I am convinced that had I found any degree of confirmation or sufferance for my kind that this coil of iron I have wound round me would now be but a decoration upon my vest. That my life would have been without shame or offence. That this very tribunal would be unnecessary."

The prosecutor smiled with malice. "Your worship, this is a song we have heard more than once. Stand down, sir, it is old news."

Jacob shouted back, "I stand up for my own." He realized his response and then said more kindly, "Sir, you are for your kind, and as you are, we will have the same deep heartfelt, self-sacrificing love for one. Yet for us, the only possible recipient of this love is a person like ourself. Is there not precedence for this? Did Shakespeare not have attachments of this kind? What of Alexander, Fredrick the Great, Leonardo, or Lilith? Did not His only son allow the disciple John to lie upon His breast? Love is as it is and regardless of its object is beautiful. Why crush it by censure and malice? Is there so much of it that we need to deny it when we find it because it is not of the norm?"

"And what of yours, Jacob Marley? What was your benefit in this?"

"I am content. Even though mine was an unrequited love it was an emotion spent nonetheless. Were I not to have given of myself would be the pity, so there is no loss in this."

The judge leaned in. "Contempt? You said you are in contempt?"

"No, your honor, I said content. And in this I am so. Also in what I have said here. I will throw my cause to this jury for their good justice. They will, I pray, find for me."

There was among the jurors then a conference. They did speak together and finally hand in their verdict. Their hands held forward and thumbs turned for a total of six thumbs down and six thumbs up. It was a hung jury unable to make a decision. All eyes turned upward toward the magistrate for his tie breaking vote.

"And so it lies with me, does it?" he cackled. He sat in his chair for a moment while he thought upon the question. Then he sat forward and looked down on Jacob who still stood before him. "Jacob Marley, I have heard your well spoken argument and do see that you have found in yourself some acceptance of who your spirit be. That you are gratified with that and will be contented with your nature. Therefore..."

The judge held up his arms and just as a white cloth did appear between his fingers the Spirit that had stood beside Jacob throughout his trial held up and wrapped his dark cloak around him, spun in a circle and then stopped so that Jacob faced a new vista.

When the Spirit lowered the wrapping Jacob found himself facing a set of stairs bathed in a pale light and advancing toward the heights. He looked upward and could see that far above the steps disappeared into a white mist. At this his heart did seem to lift itself toward it. In joy he spun and brought his hands together in supplication and gratitude . Then he realized that he felt unbound. He looked down and knew he was no longer shackled, that his mighty and ponderous chains had melted away and did no more hang heavy and implacable upon his waist. The Spirit once again held out his arm and indicated to Jacob that it was his duty to travel toward the stairs and take them upward to their destination.

Jacob looked up them and far above he now saw a bright white light as welcoming to him as a mothers arms, as a gentle touch. He felt his heart fill and rejoice as he took that first step and began to climb. It also came to his ears a choir of voices singing Hallelujah's and Hosanna's. And then from this chorus he did hear a Christmas song. And it was right. He knew truly it is at Christmas that we can find new faith and, in that, forgiveness. That this was truly the season when man could begin again and walk freely on new paths toward new plains, for it is Christmas that does renew us and make us glad. And Jacob Marley was very glad indeed.

THE END

I have endeavored, as did Mr. Dickens, to write a slight story with hopefully great import. For it is only with tolerance, acceptance, and an end of hate against gays and lesbians that will, finally, make all of us free. I hope this tale will instruct and set your hearts on a new and forgiving course. And on that path you will find love and joy and truth.

Ken Lansdowne

BIBLIOGRAPHY

Graham Robb, *Strangers: Homosexual Love In The Nineteenth Century*. New York, W.W. Norton, 2004
Paul Davis, *Charles Dickens: A To Z: The Essential Reference To His Life And Work*. New York, Facts On File Inc., 1998
Charles Dickens, *A Christmas Carol: In Prose being A Ghost Story Of Christmas*, Illustrated by Mark Summers, New York. Barnes And Noble Books, 2003
Donald Thomas, *The Victorian Underworld*. New York, New York University Press, 1998
Daniel Pool, *What Jane Austen Ate And Charles Dickens Knew: From Fox Hunting to Whist - The Facts Of Daily Life In 19th Century England*, New York, Simon And Schuster, 1993
Kristine Hughes, *The Writers Guide To Everyday Life In Regency And Victorian England: From 1811-1901*, Cincinnati. Writers Digest Books, 1998

ABOUT THE BOOK DESIGN

This book is set in Garamond, a typeface designed by the French printer Jean Jannon. It is styled after Garamond's original models, from a font of Granjon, which was probably available in the middle of the sixteenth century. Fonts also used are Cursader Gothic and Calligraph421 BT., both freeware fonts from the internet.

The illustrations are culled and worked from originals published in an 1885 edition of *The Complete Works of Charles Dickens* by J.B. Lippincott & Company of Philidelphia. The chapter head illustrations are coypright free & from *A Pictorial Archive of Printers Ornaments,* a Dover Publication.

Dedicated To:
All the Gay Men and Women who still believe in Acceptance and Love and, yes, Christmas.

First Printing: 2012

Library of Congress Cataloging in Publication Data
    Jacob Marley: a fiction/ Ken Lansdowne
        p. cm.
      ISBN 0-9740853-5-9/978-0-97402853-5-7
      1. Title

Printed in USA   H Publishing